A NOTE TO PARENTS

When your children are ready to "step into reading," giving them the right books—and lots of them—is as crucial as giving them the right food to eat. **Step into Reading Books** present exciting stories and information reinforced with lively, colorful illustrations that make learning to read fun, satisfying, and worthwhile. They are priced so that acquiring an entire library of them is affordable. And they are beginning readers with an important difference—they're written on four levels.

Step 1 Books, with their very large type and extremely simple vocabulary, have been created for the very youngest readers. **Step 2 Books** are both longer and slightly more difficult. **Step 3 Books,** written to mid-second-grade reading levels, are for the child who has acquired even greater reading skills. **Step 4 Books** offer exciting nonfiction for the increasingly proficient reader.

Children develop at different ages. **Step into Reading Books,** with their four levels of reading, are designed to help children become good—and interested—readers *faster*. The grade levels assigned to the four steps—preschool through grade 1 for Step 1, grades 1 through 3 for Step 2, grades 2 and 3 for Step 3, and grades 2 through 4 for Step 4—are intended only as guides. Some children move through all four steps very rapidly; others climb the steps over a period of several years. These books will help your child "step into reading" in style!

For
David Rudomin Hautzig
with love

Text copyright © 1995 by Random House. Illustrations copyright © 1995 by Kathy Mitchell. All rights reserved under International and Pan-American Copyright Conventions. Published in the United States by Random House, Inc., New York, and simultaneously in Canada by Random House of Canada Limited, Toronto.

Library of Congress Cataloging-in-Publication Data
Hautzig, Deborah.
Beauty and the Beast / [retold] by Deborah Hautzig.
  p. cm. — (Step into reading. A Step 3 book)
SUMMARY: Through her great capacity to love, a kind and beautiful maid releases a handsome prince from the spell which has made him an ugly beast.
ISBN 0-679-85296-4 (trade) — ISBN 0-679-95296-9 (lib. bdg.)
[1. Fairy tales. 2. Folklore—France.]
I. Beauty and the beast. II. Title. III. Series: Step into reading. Step 3 book.
PZ8.H2944Be 1995
398.2'1'0944—dc20 93-34694

Manufactured in the United States of America 10 9 8 7 6 5 4 3 2 1

STEP INTO READING is a trademark of Random House, Inc.

Step into Reading™

Beauty and the Beast

A Step 3 Book

by Deborah Hautzig

illustrated by Kathy Mitchell

Random House New York

ong ago, there lived a rich merchant who had three daughters. The youngest was so lovely that everybody called her "Beauty."

Beauty's sisters were silly and vain. They cared only about parties and money and fine clothes. They laughed at Beauty because she spent her time reading books.

But Beauty didn't mind. Unlike her
sisters, she was kind and gentle.

Then one day, the merchant lost his
fortune. With tears in his eyes, he told his
daughters that they must leave their grand
life behind them. And so they went to live
in a small country house, far from town.

Every morning, Beauty got up early. She swept and scrubbed and cooked and sewed. After her work was done, she read, or played the piano and sang.

But her sisters did nothing but complain.

"Think of all the parties we are missing!" they would cry. "Think of all

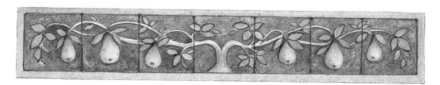

our rich friends! Beauty, you are so stupid.
How can you clean and sing and be happy
in this awful place?"

One day, the merchant had to go on a journey. Beauty's sisters were very excited!

"Bring us new dresses," they begged. "And hats and hair ribbons and jewels!"

Beauty knew her father was ~~now~~ poor and could not buy such things. So she asked for something very simple.

"Perhaps you can bring me a rose?" she said.

"You shall have your rose," said the good merchant. Then he set off on his trip.

On his way home, the merchant rode through a deep, dark forest. Suddenly, a storm hit. The rain poured down. It turned into blinding snow. Powerful winds nearly knocked the poor merchant off his horse. Wolves howled all around him.

"How will I ever get out alive?" he cried.

Suddenly, he saw lights! It was a palace! The merchant struggled through the storm toward the lights.

The great front door of the palace
stood open.

"Hello!" he called. "Is anyone here?"

No one answered.

Fearfully, the merchant stepped inside.
In the main hall, a fire crackled in the
fireplace. A table was laid out with bread
and cheese and fruit. It was as if someone
had been expecting him!

He dried himself by the fire and waited.
Perhaps the master of the house would
appear. But no one did. Finally, the
merchant was so hungry he ate all the food.

Then he made his way upstairs. The
long, dark halls were empty. The only
sounds were the echoes of his own
footsteps. But the merchant was too
exhausted to be afraid. He chose one of
the many fine bedrooms and fell into bed.

The merchant awoke the next morning and rubbed his eyes. On the table beside his bed, a cup of cocoa steamed. Over by the fire, his clothes had been laid out. Someone had cleaned them during the night!

"This palace must belong to some kind fairy who felt sorry for me," he said. "Thank you, whoever you are!"

He eagerly drank the cocoa. Then he put on his suit and prepared to leave.

As he passed through the courtyard, the merchant saw a rosebush in the garden.

He gazed at the flowers and thought of
Beauty.

Beauty was so like a rose—so tender and
beautiful! He picked a perfect rose for her.

Instantly, he heard
an angry ROAR!

A frightful creature appeared before him. "I opened my home to you!" roared the Beast. "I gave you food and drink.

I saved you from death. In return, you steal from me! You will pay for this with your LIFE!"

The merchant shook with fear and fell to his knees.

"I only wanted a rose for one of my daughters. Please, please forgive me!" he begged.

The Beast stared in silence. Then he said, "I will forgive you and let you go. But on one condition. You must send me one of your daughters. If none will come, then *you* must return."

"I promise!" said the merchant.

Once home, the merchant wept as he told his daughters about the Beast.

"This is your fault, Beauty!" cried her sisters. "You tried to show how sweet you are by asking for nothing but a rose. And now Father will die for it!"

But Beauty said, "Don't cry, Father. I will go to the Beast."

"No!" said her father. "I will go. I am old. My life is nearly over. You are still young. I will not let you go!"

"You cannot stop me, Father," said Beauty. "I love you. I will be happy to save your life!"

Beauty's wicked sisters rubbed their eyes with onions to make themselves cry when Beauty left. But they were secretly glad to see her go.

Beauty made the journey through the
deep, dark forest to the palace of the Beast.

Bravely, she opened the front door. He was waiting for her. She trembled at the sight of him.

"What will happen to me now?" thought Beauty.

But the Beast did not harm her. He spoke quietly, saying, "You are very kind to come here. The palace is yours. Do whatever you wish."

Beauty was surprised. "How gently he speaks," she thought.

His eyes, too, seemed gentle. Still, he was an ugly creature, and Beauty was afraid.

"Thank you," she said softly.

Beauty explored the palace. Each room was finer than the last.

She was amazed to come upon a door with her name on it. She opened the door and gasped.

"What a lovely room!" she cried.

Indeed it was. Best of all were the bookcases filled with thousands of books.

Beauty chose a book and opened it. In gold letters, it said:

Welcome, Beauty, banish fear.
You are Queen and mistress here:
Speak your wishes, speak your will.
Every wish we shall fulfill.

Beauty sighed. "My only wish is to see my father," she said. Instantly, her father appeared in the large mirror before her. He looked so very sad! How she longed to be with him!

As the sun set, Beauty went to the great hall. She sat down at the long table. When the Beast entered, she trembled.

"Beauty, may I dine with you?" asked the Beast.

"If you wish," whispered Beauty.

"No," said the Beast. "You are mistress here. If you want me to leave, I will. I know you find me very ugly."

"I do," said Beauty. "But I can also see that you are kind and gentle."

"My heart may be good. But I am still a monster," said the Beast sadly.

"No," said Beauty. "You are only a monster if you do evil things."

The Beast looked at her with his gentle eyes. "If I am not a monster…will you marry me?" he asked.

Beauty pulled back. "I cannot," she said.

The Beast hung his head. "Good night
then, Beauty," he said.

Beauty spent many months in the palace. Each evening she spent with the Beast. They ate, and took walks in the garden, and looked at the stars. They spoke of many things. She read to the Beast and played music for him. The better

Beauty came to know the Beast, the less she saw his ugliness.

Every night, the Beast said, "Beauty, will you marry me?"

Beauty would reply, "No, but I will always be your friend."

Every night, when the Beast said good
night, he gave her a beautiful rose.

Looking at the rose, she thought of her
father. And how she missed him. One day,
she could stand it no longer.

"Please, let me visit him," Beauty begged.

The Beast sighed miserably. "If you leave me, I will die of a broken heart!" he said.

"I never want to hurt you," said Beauty. "Let me go for just one week. I promise to come back!"

"Very well," the Beast sighed. "I cannot stand to see you unhappy. You will be with your father when you wake tomorrow. Lay this magic ring on your table when you wish to return."

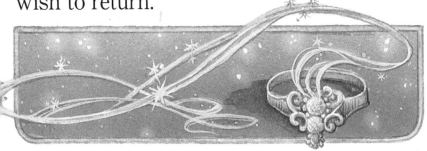

When Beauty woke up, she was at
her father's house, just as the Beast had
promised. Her father wept with joy at the
sight of her.

Beauty's sisters came to visit.

They were both married now, but they
were very unhappy. One had married a
handsome man, but he was vain and
thought only of himself. The other had
married a man who was clever and witty,
but he used his wit only to hurt his wife.

They were sick with envy to see
Beauty so happy!

"The Beast wants Beauty to come back in a week," said the oldest sister. "Let's make her stay *longer* than a week. Then the Beast will be so angry he'll eat her up!"

"Yes!" said the younger. "But how can we make her stay?"

"I have a plan," said the oldest.

After a week, Beauty was ready to leave. But her sisters wept.

"Beauty, please stay!" they cried, and tore their hair.

Beauty missed the Beast. But she also felt bad for her sisters.

"Very well," she told them. "I will stay just one more week."

The next night, Beauty had a dream.
She was in the Beast's palace. The Beast
lay in the garden. He was dying!

Beauty awoke in tears.

"My poor Beast!" she cried. "How could I break my promise to him? He is so good and tender! If he lives, I *will* marry him. If only he lives!"

Beauty quickly put the magic ring on her bedside table.

When Beauty woke up, she was back
in the Beast's palace. All day she waited
for the Beast to come to her.

But the Beast did not appear.

Beauty became more and more
worried. She searched everywhere for him,
calling, "Beast! Where are you?"

Finally, she remembered her dream. She ran to the garden.

There was the Beast, lying on the grass as if dead.

"What have I done?" cried Beauty. "Is my poor Beast dead?" She threw herself on him, weeping.

Then she heard the faint beating of his heart. He was alive!

The Beast opened his eyes.

"Beauty, you forgot your promise. You broke my heart, and now I am dying."

"No, dear Beast!" cried Beauty. "You must not die. You must live to be my husband. I will be your wife, only yours. Forever!"

At these words, something magical
happened. The dark palace burst into
light. Fireworks exploded in the sky.
Flowers bloomed. The stars sparkled as

never before, and sweet music filled the air.

Beauty looked down at the Beast she loved so much. And there before her was a handsome prince!

"My dear Beauty," said the Prince. "Now that you have broken the spell, I can tell you the truth. A wicked fairy turned me into an ugly beast. She said I would remain a beast until a beautiful lady agreed to marry me. You are the only one in the world who loved me for my true self."

Hand in hand, Beauty and the Prince went into the palace.

A good fairy appeared and said to Beauty: "Because you chose goodness over beauty, you will be a great Queen."

Then the Fairy waved her wand, and instantly Beauty's sisters appeared.

"You are wicked and mean," the Fairy told them. "Your punishment will be to watch your sister's happiness. I will turn you into statues, and you will stand in your sister's garden forever!"

With a stroke of her wand, it was done.

The Prince married Beauty. Beauty's father was the best of fathers-in-law. Beauty and the Prince lived together in the palace in great happiness for many, many years.